Biscuit's Earth Day Celebration

For everyone who
helps keep our beautiful Earth green.
—A.S.C.

by Alyssa Satin Capucilli

An Imprint of HarperCollins*Publishers*

Based on the illustration style of Pat Schories
Interior illustrations by Back Lane Studios
Biscuit's Earth Day Celebration
Text copyright © 2010 by Alyssa Satin Capucilli. Illustrations copyright © 2010 by HarperCollins Publishers.
HarperFestival is an imprint of HarperCollins Publishers. Printed in the United States of America. All rights reserved.
For information address HarperCollins Children's Books,
a division of HarperCollins Publishers, 10 East 53rd Street, New York, NY 10022.
www.harpercollinschildrens.com
Library of Congress catalog card number: 2009922235
ISBN 978-0-06-162514-5
10 11 12 13 14   UG   10 9 8 7 6 5 4 3 2 1

"Wake up, Biscuit.
It's Earth Day!"
Woof, woof!

"It's a beautiful spring day, and we have lots to do."

"We've learned a lot about Earth Day at school, Biscuit.
Today we are going to have a great celebration.
Best of all, you can come along."
Woof, woof!

"Let's get ready to go!"
Woof!

"On Earth Day we celebrate ways to take good care of our world, Biscuit. Saving water is one way we can help.

See, Biscuit?
I must turn off the water when I brush my teeth.
I don't want to waste a drop!"
Woof, woof!

"On Earth Day, it's important to help all creatures big and small, Biscuit."
Woof, woof!

"Sweet puppy!
Those twigs are just what the birds need to build a nest.
We can leave some birdseed, too."
Woof!

"Come along, Biscuit.
The celebration
is about to begin."
Woof, woof!

"We're all going to plant a garden.
We can plant flowers,
vegetables, and even trees!"
Woof, woof!
"That's the way to dig, Biscuit."
Woof!

"With lots of sunshine and water,
our seeds will grow and grow."
Woof, woof!

"Good, Biscuit! You found the watering can.
You found a wiggly worm, too!"
Woof, woof!

"This way, Biscuit.
It's time for our clean-up walk.
We can pick up paper and litter
to keep the woods
nice and clean."
Woof, woof!

"Biscuit, what have you found now?"
Woof!

"Oh no, Biscuit! Not a big shake!"
Woof, woof!
"Funny puppy!
You are keeping the pond clean, too."

"Look, Biscuit.
I decorated a bag especially for Mom and Dad
to carry groceries. They can use it again and again.
That's called recycling.

Can you tell which bag is mine?"
Woof, woof!

"This Earth Day celebration is lots of fun, Biscuit.
We can sing songs and share snacks."
Woof, woof!

"We can learn even more ways
to keep our planet safe for everyone."
Woof, woof!

Woof!
"Wait, Biscuit!
Where are you going now?"
Woof, woof!

"Hooray, Biscuit!
We can be good helpers on Earth Day..."
Woof, woof!
"...and every day!"
Woof!